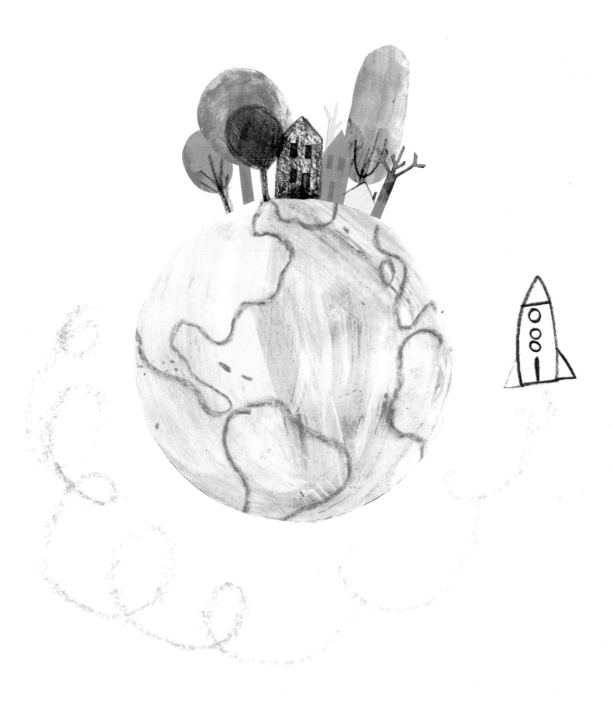

For Arthur Wilmot
and his MARVELLOUS
mummy, Lynne – S.B.

For Jenna – J.

ODD BODS

STEVEN BUTLER JARVIS

PUFFIN

AVA
is an *odd bod*.

BORIS

is too . . .

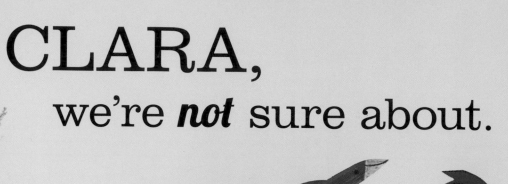

CLARA,
we're *not* sure about.

I think she's odd, **don't** you?

WHOOSH

DUNCAN'S
NEVER *trimmed* his nails.

FRANKLYN is *magnetic*

and he picks up
clips and *pins*.

AAARGH

GERTRUDE *swoops*
and ***loop-de-loops***
in circles round her room.

HERMIONE *sneaks* out at night to *howl* at the full moon.

IRIS
bends
the
teaspoons.

JOHNNY

gripes and bickers.

KITTY gets in trouble LOTS
for *flashing* folks her knickers.

LARRY'S
FULL of bogeys.

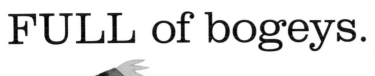

MATHILDA'S
sprung a leak.

and PERCY
just won't *speak*.

QUENTIN
moves things with his *mind*.

RAMONA
doesn't
blink.

The last time we saw
STANLEY,

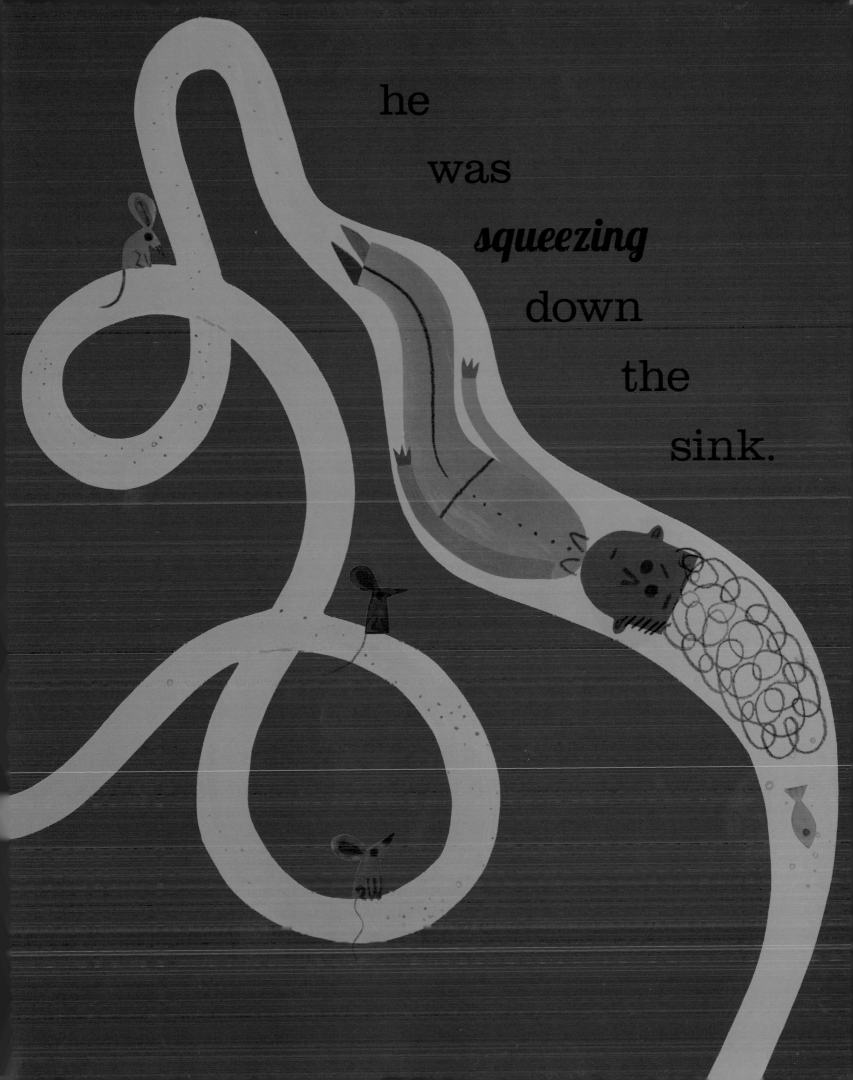

he

was

squeezing

down

the

sink.

TESSY *lifts* the family car.

UNA'S *joined* to VICKY.

and
YASMINE'S
slightly
sticky.

NO FISHING

Then there's little ZELDA,
a *sweet*, mild-mannered tot.

She
reads,

she *skips*,

she's
good
at
sports

AND . . .

CLASS 2B

PUFFIN BOOKS

UK | USA | Canada | Ireland | Australia | India | New Zealand | South Africa

Puffin Books is part of the Penguin Random House group of companies
whose addresses can be found at global.penguinrandomhouse.com.

puffinbooks.com

First published 2016

001

A CIP catalogue record for this book is available from the British Library

Printed in China

ISBN: 978–0–141–36242–7

MIX
Paper from
responsible sources
FSC
www.fsc.org   FSC® C018179